Copyright © 2001 by Nord-Süd Verlag AG, Gossau Zürich, Switzerland
First publishcd in Switzerland under the title *Oskar der kleine Elefant haut ab!*
English translation copyright © 2001 by North-South Books Inc.

First published in the United States, Great Britain, Canada,
Australia, and New Zealand in 2001 by North-South Books,
an imprint of Nord-Süd Verlag AG, Gossau Zürich, Switzerland

Distributed in the United States by North-South Books Inc., New York

Library of Congress Cataloging-in-Publication Data is available.
The CIP catalogue record for this book is available from The British Library.
ISBN 0-7358-1444-9 (trade binding)
1 3 5 7 9 TB 10 8 6 4 2
ISBN 0-7358-1445-7 (library binding)
1 3 5 7 9 LB 10 8 6 4 2
Printed in Belgium

For more information about our books, and the authors and artists
who create them, visit our web site: www.northsouth.com

Little Elephant Runs Away

By Wolfram Hänel

Illustrated by Cristina Kadmon

Translated by J. Alison James

North-South Books

New York / London

The little elephant was angry.
First his big sister had taken all his bananas.
And when he almost started to cry, she'd laughed
at him. And then his big brother called him a
crybaby and kicked him. On purpose!

"Everyone is mean to me," the little elephant complained to his mother. "But I'm not going to take it anymore. I'm running away."

"Go right ahead," said his mother. "But don't go too far. It's already late."

She didn't even listen to what I said, thought the little elephant. Nobody takes me seriously. I really am going to run away. I'll go to the sea and never come back.

The little elephant went down to the river. His sister and brother were in the water spraying each other. But the little elephant pretended they weren't there and walked on.

All rivers go to the sea. So the little elephant only had to follow the river and he'd reach the sea before long. It was as simple as that.

The little elephant ran at first, so he could get far away from his brother and sister as fast as possible.

After a while the little elephant slowed down
and started to notice things. He saw a giraffe
who was nibbling a couple of leaves from high
up in a tree. What a long neck she has! thought
the little elephant, amazed.

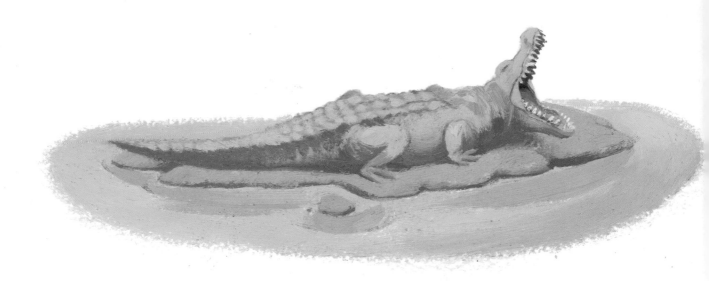

A crocodile lay on a sandbar. He opened his mouth in a wide yawn. What sharp teeth he has! thought the little elephant.

Then he saw a pair of zebras, who had come to the river to drink. They looked so silly, the little elephant thought, and he had to laugh.

The little elephant was hot, so he left the river
and wandered into the jungle. After that he didn't
see any other animals. Of course there were animals
here, but they were hidden. The little elephant could
hear them. From all around him came sounds of
whispering and rustling and crackling. . . .

I am louder than they are, the little elephant
thought. He raised his trunk and trumpeted.
"Terooot!" went the little elephant. The strange noise
frightened a small monkey so much that he toppled
out of a tree.

"I'm sorry," the little elephant said, but the monkey
had already disappeared.

It was nice and cool in the forest, the little elephant
decided. His sister was nowhere near to take his
bananas. And his brother was too far away to kick
him. The little elephant lifted his trunk again and
went: *"Toot-toot-teroot!"*

    The little elephant was growing tired. The sea was nowhere to be seen, and it was turning dark. The little elephant had never been away from home at night.

    The rustling and whispering around him grew louder and louder. The little elephant could toot as much as he wanted, it didn't help. He was afraid, and he was terribly lonely.

Surely they are looking for me by now, thought the little elephant. When they don't find me, they will start to worry. But they deserve to. They were so mean to me. Even so, it would be nice if they came to find me right about now. . . .

The little elephant decided to head back home. But when he looked around, he didn't quite remember which way he'd come. The little elephant was lost!

   If I trumpet for help, thought the little elephant,
then everyone will know I was afraid and my brother
will come running and call me a crybaby again.
What can I do? He made a quiet little *"Teroot."*
It sounded rather sad.

A pair of monkeys tumbled out of a tree and surprised the little elephant. Suddenly he had a wonderful idea. He fell down and pretended that he was sick.

The monkeys shrieked and chattered and boxed him a little in the belly. But the little elephant didn't stir. He stayed still until the chattering monkeys ran off to find help.

It wasn't long at all before his mother came trotting through the forest, followed by his brother.

"Did something happen to you?" asked his mother. "Did you fall down? Are you hurt?"

"Oh, no," said the little elephant, and he quickly jumped up to his feet. "I was on my way to the sea, but I got tired and stopped to rest."

"Whaat?" asked his brother, astonished. "You were going alone to the sea?"

"Of course," said the little elephant. "All by myself. But now that you're here, I think I'll go back home with you. The sea can wait for another day."

"Tell me," asked his brother, "could I come along when you go to the sea again?"

"Why not?" replied the little elephant. Then he marched happily home behind his mother and his brother. And every once in a while he lifted his trunk and went *"Toot-toot-teroot!"* loudly and proudly.